Bob Robber
and
Dancing Jane

For Jessica, with love
A.M.

For John O. to say thank you
B.W.

BOB ROBBER AND DANCING JANE
A RED FOX BOOK 0 09 943397 4

First published in Great Britain by Jonathan Cape
an imprint of Random House Children's Books

Jonathan Cape edition published 2003
Red Fox edition published 2004

1 3 5 7 9 10 8 6 4 2

Red Fox Books are published by Random House Children's Books,
61–63 Uxbridge Road, London W5 5SA,
a division of The Random House Group Ltd,
in Australia by Random House Australia (Pty) Ltd,
20 Alfred Street, Milsons Point, Sydney, NSW 2061, Australia,
in New Zealand by Random House New Zealand Ltd,
18 Poland Road, Glenfield, Auckland 10, New Zealand,
and in South Africa by Random House (Pty) Ltd,
Endulini, 5A Jubilee Road, Parktown 2193, South Africa

THE RANDOM HOUSE GROUP Limited Reg. No. 954009
www.kidsatrandomhouse.co.uk

A CIP catalogue record for this book is available from the British Library.

Printed in Singapore

ANDREW MATTHEWS

BOB ROBBER
AND
DANCING JANE

ILLUSTRATED BY
BEE WILLEY

RED FOX

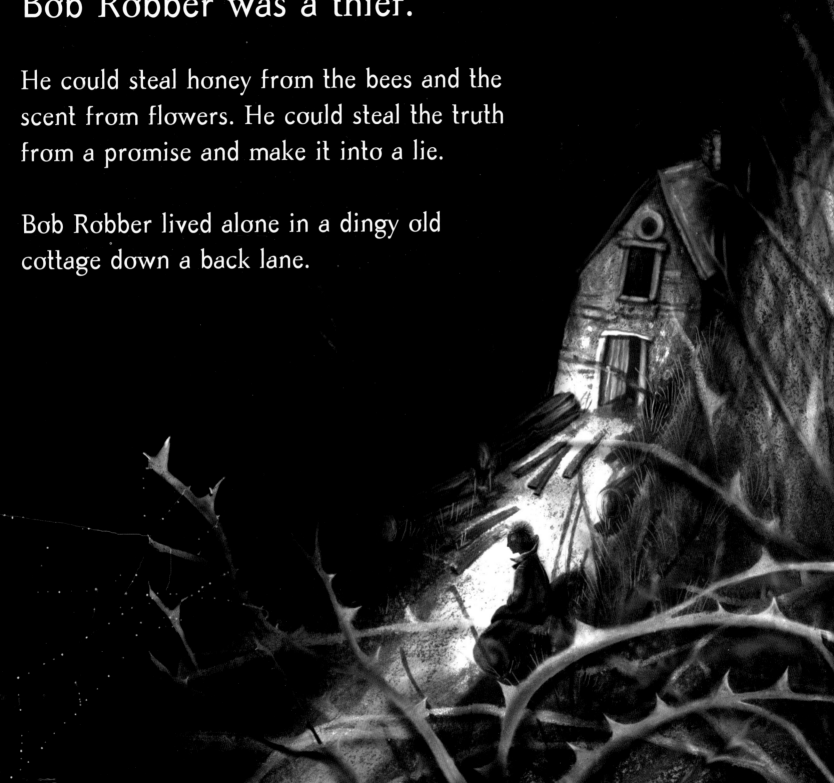

Bob Robber was a thief.

He could steal honey from the bees and the scent from flowers. He could steal the truth from a promise and make it into a lie.

Bob Robber lived alone in a dingy old cottage down a back lane.

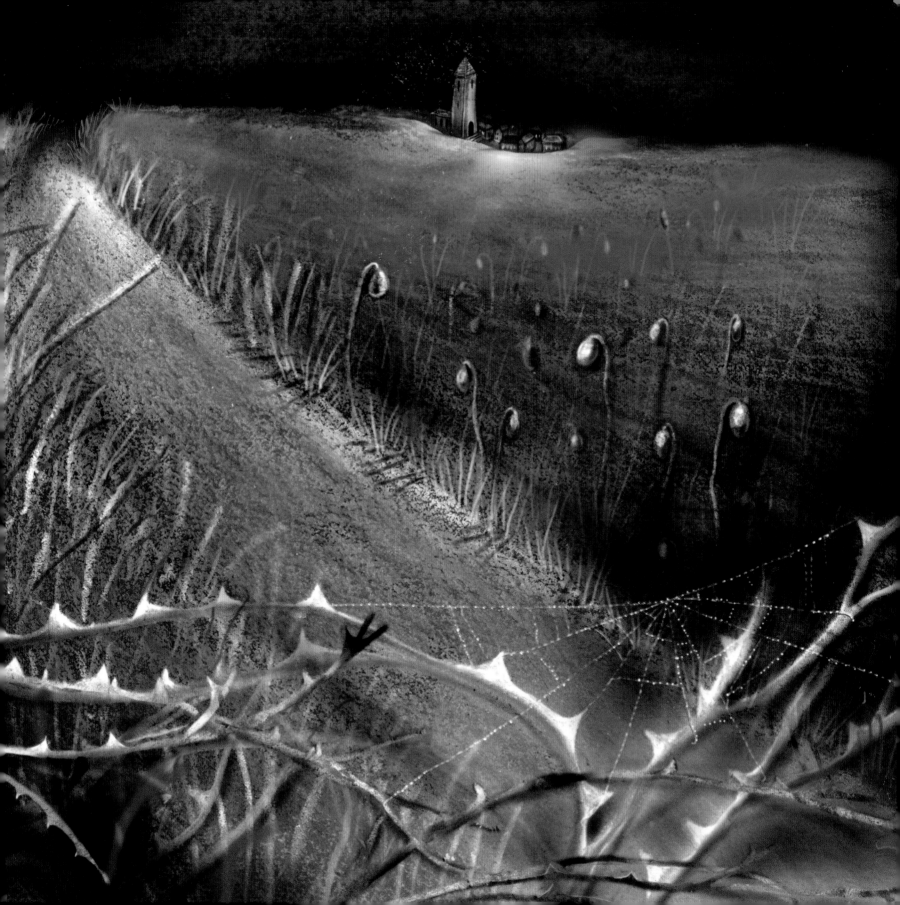

His hair was black as bats
and his eyes were the colour
of the new moon. Bob Robber
could stand so still that spiders
didn't notice him and spun
webs across his clothes. When
he moved, he was quieter than
moss. His thieving fingers
were as nimble as fish and he
could run faster than morning
to be back in his cottage
before the sun came up.

One summer night when the moon was full, Bob Robber
was waiting in the darkness at the side of the road when
Dancing Jane passed by. Her feet were light, her eyes
were brown and her dress was white as winter snow.

　As soon as he saw Dancing Jane, Bob Robber
wanted to dance with her, but he stayed in the dark.
"I can creep and I can steal, but I can't dance a step!"
he said to himself.

Dancing Jane glimpsed a shape
in the shadows and felt afraid.
"Who's there?" she called.
But Bob Robber gave
no answer. He crept
and stole his
way home.

Next night Bob Robber
waited in the same place
and Dancing Jane came
by again, singing and
dancing on her shadow.
Her feet were light, her hair
was dark and her dress was
red as autumn leaves.

Bob Robber wanted to dance
with her so much that a tear
rolled down his cheek.
"I can sneak and I can
thieve, but I can't dance
a step!" he said to himself.

Dancing Jane saw the tear
gleam in the dark and
shivered.

"Who's there?" she called.

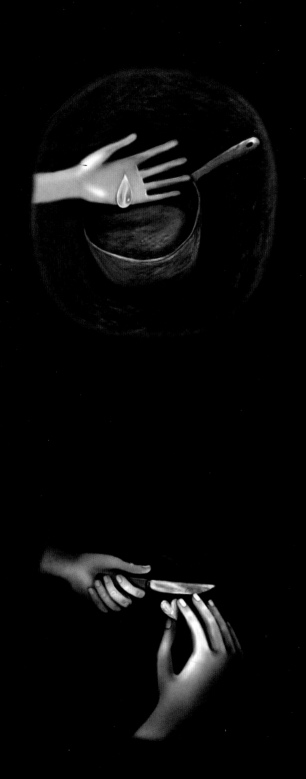

But Bob Robber made no reply. He turned away and sneaked home.

He took the tear from his cheek and left it in a cold iron pan until it was as hard and clear as glass.

Then he took a knife and carved the tear into a tiny, glittering heart.

On the third night, Bob Robber left the heart in the middle of the road and waited for Dancing Jane. As the moon rose over the hill, Dancing Jane came along, singing and dancing with her shadow. Her feet were light, her voice was sweet and her dress was blue as summer skies.

When she saw the tiny heart glittering
in the moonlight, bright as a star,
she stopped to pick it up.

"Whose heart is this?" she called.
Bob Robber slipped out of hiding,
silent as frost. He crept up
behind Dancing Jane and
stole her shadow from the
moonlit road. Then he was off,
with the shadow over his shoulder.

"Stop, thief!" shouted Dancing Jane.
But no one heard her cries for help.

When he got to
his cottage, Bob Robber
tried to dance with the shadow,
but it slid through his fingers.
It flopped and folded. It wilted and wavered
like the flame of a candle and would not dance.

"This is no good!" Bob Robber snapped.
Then he climbed his creaking, rickety stairs, locked the
shadow in a wooden chest, got into bed and fell fast asleep.

And as he slept he dreamed of Dancing Jane, sighing and sobbing as she searched for her shadow.

When Bob Robber woke at dusk, something was wrong.
He tried to move quietly, but he crashed and bumbled.
He tried to stand still, but his arms twitched.

His thieving fingers felt as stiff as sticks. "I can't
sneak and I can't creep any more," said Bob Robber.

"I gave Dancing Jane my heart, but I stole
her shadow and now I must give it back."
He went to the chest, took out the shadow and
carried it with him to wait for Dancing Jane.

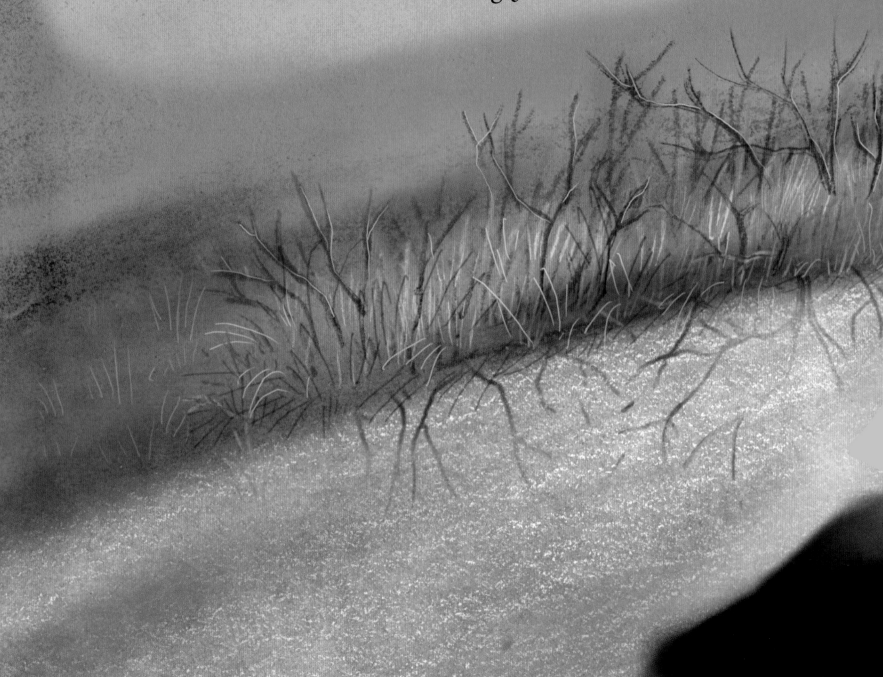

He stood in the middle of the road
and watched the rising moon. Dancing
Jane came along, walking slowly, holding
the heart in her hands. Her feet were
heavy, her eyes were sad and her dress
was grey as ashes.

She saw Bob Robber and frowned. "You're
the thief who stole my shadow and left
his heart on the road!" she said.
Bob Robber hung his head in shame.

"Last night I was a thief," he
said. "Tonight I don't know who
I am. Here is your shadow.
You can keep my heart."

Dancing Jane took back her shadow. She held up the heart so that it glittered in the light of the moon, and she began to dance.

She danced slowly at first, then faster and faster, twisting and turning around Bob Robber. She danced the cobwebs off his coat and she danced the night out of him. She danced the honey back to the bees, the scent back to the flowers and filled the darkness with unbroken promises.

Bob Robber felt his courage grow.

He stretched out his hands and for the first time in his life, he asked for something instead of stealing it. "Please teach me to dance!" he said.

So Dancing Jane took him by the hand and they danced on the road while their shadows twirled at their feet.

All night they danced and at dawn Bob Robber looked around and smiled.

"I've never seen the sun come up before," he said.

The morning was so beautiful
that Bob Robber forgot to return
to his cottage.
He danced away with Dancing Jane
and he never stole again.